THE GREAT HAMSTER RESCUE!

LILY ROSCOE AND TONY NEAL

SIMON & SCHUSTER

London   New York   Sydney   Toronto   New Delhi

Yo, kiddo, how you doin'?
My name's Rita
'Roberella' Rat,
the one and only leader
of the Rat Burglar Gang.

Let me introduce you to my team.

'MOTOR' MORTY

GINA 'GADGET' GAL

HARRY 'HOLD 'EM UP' HAMSTER

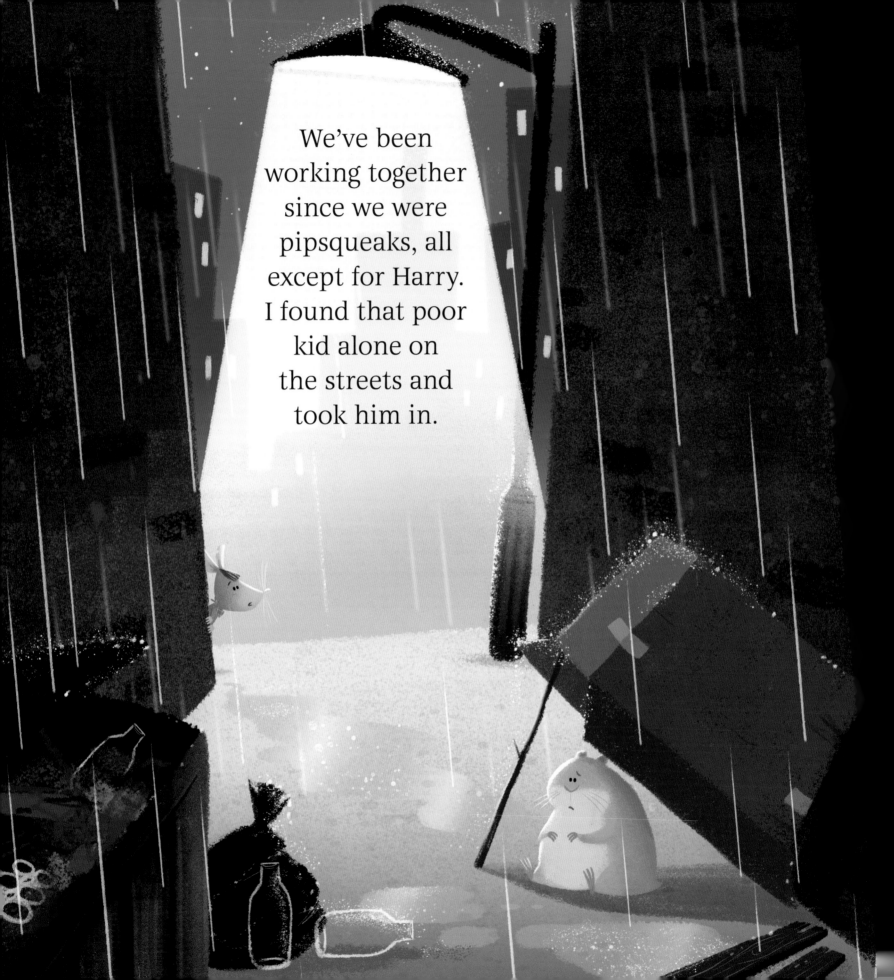

We've been working together since we were pipsqueaks, all except for Harry. I found that poor kid alone on the streets and took him in.

We four are a family, and one thing's for sure . . .
We ain't nobody's pet!

That is, until last Tuesday . . .

Picture the scene . . .
We're downtown outside Mo's
Pet Shop, waiting for a delivery
of the finest quality pet food.

Mo's Pet Sh

Harry's about to steal the stuff, when suddenly . . .

Mo looks down and mistakes the guy
for one of his own pet hamsters.

Before we have time to bite old Mo's ankle . . .

. . . He scoops up Harry and locks him in a cage.

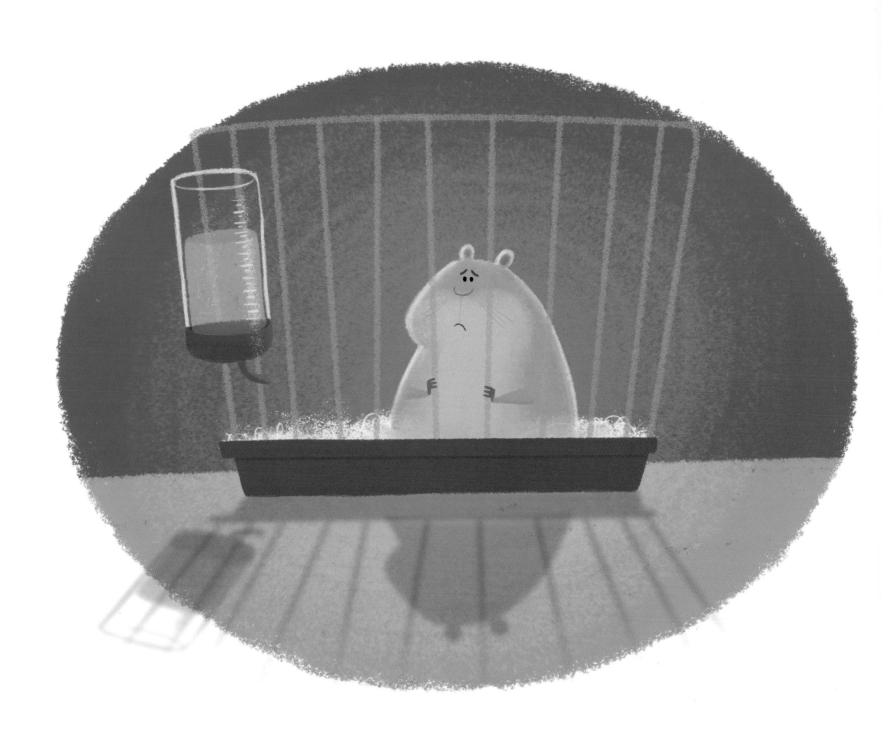

But it gets worse.

"Mummy, look, I want that one.
He is SOOOOOOOOOOOOO cute."

I'll never forget the look on poor Harry's face as the kid says,
"I'm going to call you Snuggle Puff Muffin Rainbow."

We have to save our buddy and FAST.

So we trail the little girl's car
and follow her home.

And we wait . . .

And we wait . . .

And we wait . . .

And we wait . . .

Until finally, the coast is clear.

We decide to divide and conquer.

Morty takes his place in the getaway car.

Gina shimmies up to the top floor
window to get a view inside.

The place is a FORTRESS.

But that's not going to stop us!

I scurry through the letterbox – growling, drooling robo-dogs chasing at my heels.

GGRRR! GGRRR!

I radio to Gina, asking her to stand by as back-up.

Inside the house, alarm bells are blaring, lasers are beaming, robo-dogs are barking and . . .

And just as I think
    I've escaped the last trap . . .

Luckily, Gina saves me in the nick of time.

scoop!!

Finally, we make it upstairs. Gina goes left. I go right. We run from room to room to room,

until . . .

. . . There I see him.

Hold 'Em Up Harry,
running circles in a
wheel, a pretty little bow
in his hair. He looks sad,
embarrassed, pitiful.
He looks like . . .

. . . a pet!

"Pssst . . . Harry, it's me – Rita. The gang and I have come to rescue you from that pesky little kid."

"But, Rita," Harry says, "I like that little kid. She sings me lullabies. She does my hair all pretty. She even calls me Snuggle Puff."

"But what about your freedom, Harry?! And . . . what about *us?*"

"Rita," says Harry, "I'll always love you and the guys,
but I guess I'm just a pet at heart."

"Well if you're happy then I'm happy for you,
Snuggle Puff."

"Toodle-oo, Rita."

"Toodle-oo? Man, you think you know someone
and then they turn out to be a pet."

But I guess the Rat Burglar
life can't be for everyone.
Sometimes I even question it
myself. Maybe I should retire,
change my ways, become a . . .

. . . PET?

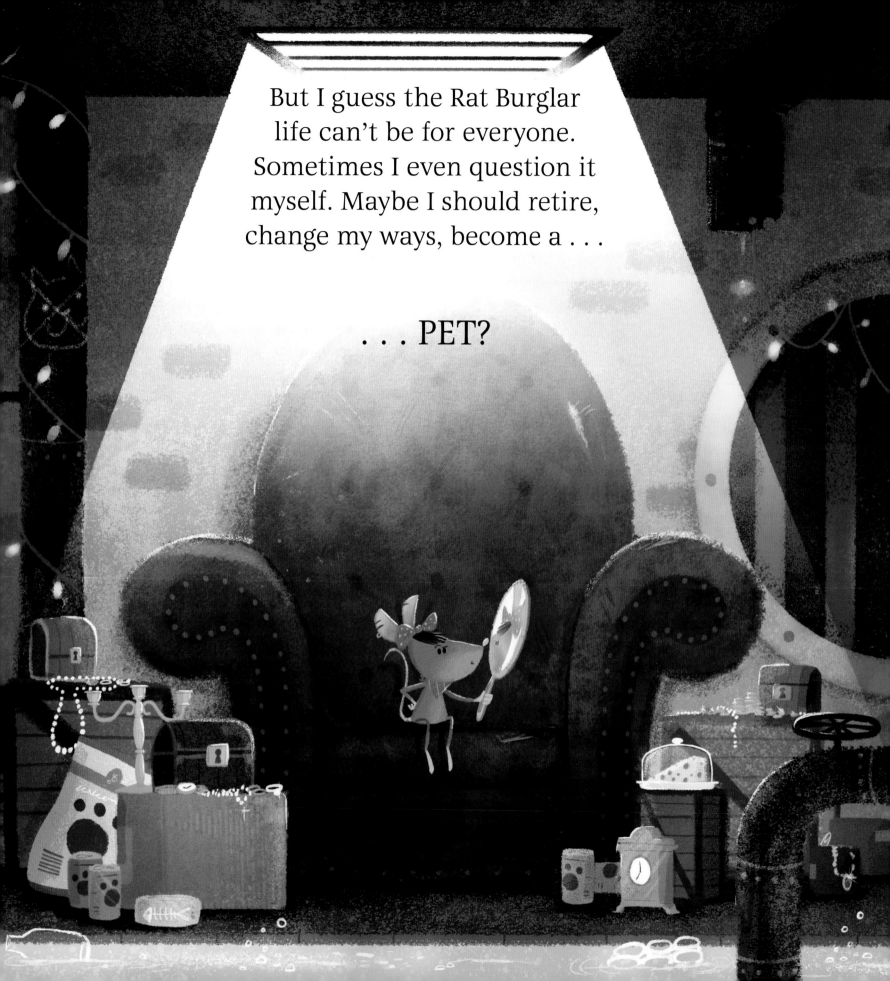

That can wait until tomorrow . . .